THE RAINFOREST EXPRESS

SEAN CALLERY

EVANS BROTHERS LIMITED

Characters

Mr Beamer a businessman
Lee his son

Jay
Ahmed
Dreena ⎤ school friends
Wanda ⎦
Chloe a fashion-mad school friend

Mrs Wills Lee's neighbour, a teacher

Mrs Hurst a teacher
Delon a school child
Sally a school child

Satnav the satellite navigation system on the bus
Astronaut
Mission control

Maria a girl in the rainforest
Gab a boy in the rainforest
Mr Dev a boss in the rainforest
Crocodiles and villagers

The Rainforest Express

Act One Scene One

*In the Beamer house, Mr Beamer unpacks
burgers and buns. Lee plays on his laptop.
The doorbell rings*

Mr Beamer: Answer the door, Lee. I'm doing the burgers.

Lee: Can't you go, Dad? I just got to the next level.

Mr Beamer: My hands are dirty. Anyway you wanted to
invite some of your friends for the barbecue,
remember? It could be them. Answer the door.

(The doorbell rings again)

Jay: *(Shouting through the letterbox)* Hello? Anybody
there?

*(A voice comes from the laptop: Game over.
Chainsaw Fighter wins by 2,000 points)*

Lee: Rats. OK, OK.

(He opens the door. Jay and Ahmed come in)

Jay: We've come to the right house, then.

Lee: Hi Jay. What car did you come in?

Jay: Ahmed's mum dropped us off. Why?

Lee: I just wanted to see what car you've got.

Ahmed: It's a VW. Are the others here yet?

Lee: Golf GTI?

Ahmed: Just a Polo.

Lee: *(Unimpressed)* Oh right. Bottom of the range. I was on Chainsaw Fighter. Do you want to see it?

Jay: Wow, cool laptop!

Lee: Yeah, it was the most expensive one they had.

Jay: Are all these games yours? There's hundreds!

Lee: Yep. Anyway, in Chainsaw Fighter there's this guy with a chainsaw and he carves people up. You have to keep moving and throw mud at him so he can't get you… Tell you what, you watch while I play and you'll pick it up.

Ahmed: *(Sadly)* Right. We'll watch then.

(Lee starts up the game. The doorbell rings)

Lee: Can you get that? It will be one of the others from school.

Ahmed: OK. I'll go. *(He goes to the door)*

Chloe: *(Calling through the letterbox)* Hello? Lee? *(She rings the doorbell again while Ahmed tries to open the door)*

Ahmed: Sorry, I can't get the door to open.

Mr Beamer: *(Comes to the door)* What's the problem? Here, let me. *(He opens the door)* Hello. Sorry to keep you waiting. I'm Mr Beamer.

Chloe: Hello, Mr Beamer. I'm Chloe.

Mr Beamer: Come on through.

Chloe: Thank you.

Mr Beamer: Where's Lee?

Ahmed: He's on his computer.

Mr Beamer: That's so rude. *(He calls into the next room)* Lee! Turn that thing off and come and talk to your friends.

Lee: *(Reluctantly turns off his laptop and emerges with Jay)* All right, all right. Hi, Chloe. Hey, like the Jungle World T-shirt.

Jay: What's Jungle World?

Chloe: It's the coolest label.

Lee: From the discount store?

Chloe: Yeah. But it's not fake. I love their stuff.

Lee: I get mine from the shop next to Dad's.

Mr Beamer: Come on you lot, go into the garden and have a drink and something from the barbie. *(As Lee passes him he whispers)* Lee, lay off about the designer gear. Not all your friends can afford that stuff. *(More loudly, to the others)* Sheesh, it's baking out here! Good old global warming, eh? I love these hot summers.

Chloe: Can I have a Coke?

Mr Beamer: Take anything you want. Fancy a drink, lads?

(The doorbell rings. Mr Beamer looks at Lee, who goes to answer it)

Jay: Anything except water. I hate water.

Chloe: That fizzy stuff in the blue bottles is OK.

Ahmed: Tap water is fine for me. *(Whispering to Chloe)* He shouldn't be pleased about global warming. It's killing the planet.

Chloe: *(Absently)* Yeah, whatever. *(Enthusiastically)* Have you seen how much designer stuff they've got? Look, even the barbecue charcoal is Jungle World.

Jay: Yeah, it's pretty smart here.

(Dreena comes in with Wanda)

Dreena: Hi, you lot.

Chloe: Hi, Dreena. Look how posh Lee's place is.

Ahmed: Seen that massive patio heater? It's crazy. It just heats up the sky.

Chloe: And the barbie's bigger than my bedroom!

Dreena: Yeah, but I bet there's nothing I can eat on it.

Jay: Why not?

Chloe: *(Rolls her eyes)* She's gone vegetarian. Dreena's latest fad. 'Save the planet', 'Stop killing whales', and now 'Meat is murder'. Isn't that right, Dreen?

Dreena: Well at least I think about more than the latest designer label.

Ahmed: I don't eat meat either, Dreena, but there are veggie burgers.

Dreena: Great, cheers Ahmed. *(She serves herself while she talks)* I like them with lots of sauce. Hold my plate, Chloe, so I can give it a good squirt. *(She squirts tomato ketchup at her plate, splashing it onto Chloe's T-shirt and even hitting the door behind her)*

Chloe: You did that on purpose! It's ruined!

Dreena: I so did not. It was an accident, wasn't it Jay? You saw.

Jay: Well…

Mr Beamer: What's this? You've got ketchup all over the decking. It'll stain. They only fitted it yesterday and I haven't varnished the wood yet. Lee! Get a cloth!

Dreena: I'm really sorry. I didn't mean to.

Chloe: Yeah, right. That was my best T-shirt.

Scene Two

Mrs Wills calls over the garden fence

Mrs Wills: Excuse me? I'm sorry to interrupt your party.

Mr Beamer: What's up?

Mrs Wills: There's a car blocking my drive.

Mr Beamer: Can't you just park in the road for now?

Mrs Wills: I would if I could. This is going to sound really silly, but my van grew this morning and now it's too big to leave on the road.

Mr Beamer: Grew?

Mrs Wills: Yes. I used to have a little camper van.

Lee: I've seen that. *(To Jay, quietly)* It's so old and bashed up. I wouldn't use it for a toilet.

Mr Beamer: I've got a mate who sells cars. He'll do you a good deal.

Mrs Wills: No thank you, this one suits me fine. Anyway, this morning it turned into a bus!

Mr Beamer: You what?

Mrs Wills: It's got the same number plate and it's still green, except it has flowers painted on it. The old key still works, but it is definitely a bus. It's as if my little van grew up!

Mr Beamer: You should report it.

Mrs Wills: Who to? I don't know who to call when a van grows. Anyway, I quite like it. I got in and the engine started and it seemed to know where to go.

Mr Beamer: I beg your pardon?

Mrs Wills: I was taking some old clothes to the charity shop. And it took me to the door. I hardly had to do a thing!

Mr Beamer: I'd get that looked at if I were you.

Mrs Wills: Oh I don't know. I sort of want to see what it will do next. Anyway, it's too wide to park in the road so can you move the car that's in the way?

Lee: What is it?

Chloe: *(Looking past the house up the drive)* A BMW.

Lee: That's Wanda's dad's car. I'll tell him. *(He leaves)*

Mrs Wills: Thank you. Enjoy your barbecue. Bye! *(She leaves)*

Mr Beamer: Yep. Lovely. Cheerio. *(More quietly)* Mad old hippy. What planet is she on? *(The bus engine starts up)* That old rustbucket makes a lot of noise, too.

Lee: *(Returns)* And it's got stupid flowers painted all over it.

(Exit)

SCENE THREE

Next day. Mrs Hurst and all the schoolchildren are in the classroom

Mrs Hurst: *(Grimacing)* Oh, my poor head. Sorry, children. Where were we?

Wanda: When will the bus be here?

Mrs Hurst: The swimming bus! I think I forgot to book it!

(The children groan with disappointment)

Ahmed, go and ask in the office and see if they know.

Ahmed: OK, Mrs Hurst. *(He leaves)*

(Jay puts his hand up)

15

Mrs Hurst: You haven't forgotten your kit again, Jay?

Jay: Yes. Sorry, Mrs Hurst.

Lee: You so didn't forget! I saw you dump it in the hedge outside school.

Jay: I didn't!

Lee: You've done it before. You hate going swimming and you're always 'forgetting' your kit.

Jay: Maybe. It's really hard. I can't breathe properly and I get in a panic.

Mrs Hurst: OK class, let's work together to help here. What could Jay do to help himself with his swimming?

Wanda: Bring his kit for a start, so that he has a lesson and learns to keep his feet up and kick.

Jay: I know about that, and keeping your fingers together. I just can't do it properly.

Lee: I learned to swim when my dad said he'd pay me to do it.

Mrs Hurst: Right, so it might be a question of motivation. Maybe Jay needs to find a really good reason to swim. It might help him.

Chloe: *(Picking her nails)* Well I don't mind if we miss swimming today.

Mrs Hurst: Why not? You're a good swimmer, Chloe.

Chloe: It might sound silly but I'm quite fussy about how I look–

Dreena: Yes, we had noticed!

Chloe: And I don't want to go swimming today because I've got a wart on my foot and it looks gross.

Wanda: She shouldn't worry because no one's paying any attention.

Mrs Hurst: Rather like you, Wanda. Can you come away from the window, please?

Dreena: Well I was quite looking forward to going swimming. I'm not scared like Jay – the only thing I'm scared of is crocodiles – and there's none of those there!

(The class laugh)

Don't laugh! They freak me out.

Mrs Hurst: Why do they freak you out, Dreena?

Dreena: They just do. You know I'm really good at staring matches? The ones where the first one to blink loses.

Sally: Yeah, she is. I tried to beat her once and I had a headache for days.

Dreena: Anyway, I was at the zoo and we got to the reptile house, and there was this creepy, knobbly crocodile. And I thought, 'I'm not scared of you,' and started a staring match with it. I didn't stand a chance. It gave me this long, horrible look and all I could think was, 'It's going to eat me.'

Chloe: *(Sings)* Never smile at a crocodile, no you can't get friendly with a crocodile….

Mrs Hurst: Thank you, Chloe, we don't do music until this afternoon.

Ahmed: *(Returns)* They said the coach hasn't been booked and now it is too late.

(The children groan, apart from Jay)

Mrs Hurst: Thanks, Ahmed. Children, I'm so sorry about that. And now my headache has got so much worse, I'm going to have to go and lie down. You'll have to mix in with Mr Jackman's class.

Wanda: So we're definitely not going swimming?

Sally: But I was going to do the diving test today!

Mrs Hurst: We'll do it next week. Wanda, will you please come away from the window?

Wanda: Wow. That's a cool bus! It must have been booked after all!

(The class rushes to the window)

Mrs Hurst: Who's that lady? Why is that bus in the playground?

Lee: She's got out. That bus is parking itself!

Mrs Hurst: Are you sure?

Lee: Oh, I know her. That's Mrs Wills from next door. My dad says she's barmy – you know, short of a few brain cells.

Chloe: A few sandwiches short of a picnic!

Wanda: A few fries short of a Happy Meal!

Jay: A few trees short of a forest!

Mrs Hurst: That's enough. She's coming in. Be nice.

Mrs Wills: *(Enters)* Good morning, everyone.

Mrs Hurst: Good morning. Mrs Wills, isn't it?

Mrs Wills: Yes, were you expecting me?

Mrs Hurst: What do you mean?

Mrs Wills: Well, it's the strangest thing. I got in my bus this morning and I was going to do some supply teaching at Southwold School – the one across town. My bus has one of those things that tells you how to get somewhere.

Lee: A satnav.

Mrs Wills: Yes. When I turned it on it brought me here instead. The bus stopped and the voice said, 'Go to Mrs Hurst's class, they are expecting you.' So here I am.

Dreena: So you're a teacher?

Mrs Wills: Yes.

Dreena: And you've got a bus?

Mrs Wills: Well, yes.

Dreena: Fantastic! Mrs Hurst, you can stay here. We've got a proper teacher and a bus to take us to the swimming pool!

Mrs Hurst: I often wonder why you aren't in charge here already, Dreena.

Dreena: Why, thank you, Miss!

Mrs Hurst: That looks like a very good idea. It means you can all go swimming and I can stay here to nurse my headache.

Jay: I can't go swimming: I haven't got any kit.

Mrs Wills: Ah, you must be Jay.

Jay: How did you know?

Mrs Wills: The voice – what is it?

Lee: Satnav.

Mrs Wills: Yes, Satnav told me there was spare kit and towels in the front of the bus for someone called Jay. It said it knew your size. So you'll be fine!

Jay: *(Disappointed)* Oh… great.

Exit

Scene Four

The children and Mrs Wills are on the bus

Mrs Wills: Is everybody strapped in?

Children: Yes.

Mrs Wills: Has everybody got their swimming stuff?

Children: Yes.

Jay: No.

Dreena: Good job we sat at the front. Here are the spares by the driver's seat. There will be something here that fits you, and there are nice fluffy towels, too.

Jay: *(Without enthusiasm)* Great.

Mrs Wills: Who knows the way to the pool?

Dreena: Why can't you use the satnav?

Mrs Wills: Oh yes, silly me. *(She talks to Satnav)* Take us to the pool. *(The bus doesn't move)* Oh, that's right. It was like this earlier on. You have to be very polite to it. *(To Satnav)* Please will you take us to the pool?

(The engine starts and the bus sets off)

Wanda: Don't we go left at this roundabout?

Ahmed: Hey, we missed the turning.

Sally: The pool is THAT way!

Mrs Wills: I'm getting a bit confused here.

Sally: Why is it taking us the wrong way?

Ahmed: Try turning left again and again….

Wanda: We've gone in a big circle.

Ahmed: That's our school!

Sally: Delon's feeling sick, Miss!

Mrs Wills: I'll stop. *(She stops the bus and turns off the engine)* We can sort Delon out and decide which way to go. *(She walks down the aisle towards Delon with the sick bucket)*

(The engine starts)

Wanda: What's happening?

(The bus starts moving)

Sally: This is scary.

Ahmed: I can't look!

Mrs Wills: Mind that bucket!

(The sick bucket rolls down the bus)

Lee: Eurgh.

Jay: Gross.

(The bus soars into the air)

Wanda: We've taken off.

Lee: We're flying!

Sally: That's the pool down there. We've gone into some clouds.

Mrs Wills: *(Trying to use her mobile phone)* My mobile phone isn't working.

Wanda: I can't see anything.

Mrs Wills: I can't get a signal.

Satnav: Welcome aboard the Rainforest Express. We will be going on a climate change tour. Enjoy the trip.

Everyone: Argh!

Jay: Well at least we're not going swimming. Excellent. But how are we going to get back? No one is in charge of the bus.

Mrs Wills: I'm sorry, children, we'll just have to see where the bus takes us. I hope it knows what it's doing.

Satnav: Relax, sit down and enjoy the ride, Molly.

Chloe: Hey, Mrs Hurst is called Molly!

Mrs Wills: How did it know my name?

Satnav: If you see somewhere you'd like to land, you only have to ask.

Lee: Land now, then, you stupid robot.

(The bus flies on)

Satnav: But of course you have to ask nicely, Lee.

Wanda: I can see ice!

Jay: We can go skating instead of swimming! Could we go down here, please?

Satnav: Since you ask so nicely, Jay, yes we can. Hold on tight everybody. This is going to be quite a steep dive.

(The bus dives)

Everyone: Argh!

Lee: I want my mum!

Scene Five

The bus has landed on the Arctic ice

Jay: This isn't the skating rink. Where are we?

Wanda: All I can see out there is ice.

Chloe: It's like we're on top of a wedding cake.

Dreena: We're on top of the world. I don't know how but we've gone a very long way.

Ahmed: I think I've seen this on the telly. Excuse me, Satnav, but is this the Arctic, please?

Satnav: Yes, Ahmed.

Mrs Wills: Wow, the Arctic. Let's get out and have a look.

Satnav: Please read out the safety instructions on my display before you go out. Use the microphone so that the people at the back can hear.

Jay: *(Using the bus microphone)* Put on all your clothes, including hats and gloves. Don't eat chocolate as it will freeze and break your teeth.

Sally: Not fair! I was saving a piece of chocolate for after the swim.

Satnav: There are more instructions on my display.

Jay: *(Reading)* If the ice cracks, get on the bus. If you see a polar bear, say your prayers.

Chloe: Still, there are no crocodiles, so you'll be all right, Dreena!

Dreena: Very funny.

Mrs Wills: OK, let's go and have a look.

(They get off the bus)

Lee: I wish I had a snowmobile, or a sledge pulled by huskies.

Jay: Hey, watch this. *(He spits at the ground)*

Lee: Wow! It freezes before it lands!

Jay: Awesome! Let's make a spit mountain!

(Mrs Wills watches Lee and Jay enthusiastically spit on the ice)

Mrs Wills: I knew there was a reason why I stopped teaching full time.

Dreena: I just saw a seal!

(There is a crash a long way away)

Jay: What was that?

Mrs Wills: Look on the horizon, as far as you can see. That looks like a mountain but actually it's a glacier.

Jay: Yeah, I see.

Mrs Wills: That's a frozen river. Part of it just fell into the sea. The glaciers are melting.

(There is a loud cracking sound)

Chloes: What was that? Another glacier?

Jay: No, look by your feet. The ice is cracking!

Mrs Wills: Quick, everyone, get back on the bus.

(They rush back on)

Wanda: I can see water on both sides of us.

Dreena: The ice has cracked around the bus and we're floating.

Chloe: Oh yeah, an ice floe, and there's another one over there with a polar bear on it.

Wanda: Wait a sec. Polar bears are white, and that ice is red.

Chloe: I think the red stuff is what is left of Dreena's seal.

Ahmed: Gross, man!

Lee: That is cool!

Dreena: Not cool for the seal.

Jay: What made the ice crack?

Dreena: I read about this. It's because of climate change. The Arctic ice is cracking and melting faster and faster.

Ahmed: That's right. The polar bears have got less and less ice to live on, because so much is floating away. They're short of food.

Lee: Well that one seemed to manage. Look, he's ripped the seal's guts out! It's like a scene from Chainsaw Fighter.

Jay: Yeah, but for real. That could be us, Lee.

Chloe: We should get out of here.

Mrs Wills: Please, Satnav, take us away from here.

(The bus honks its horn and soars into the air)

Thank you.

Chloe: Am I the only person who thinks we could have got killed then?

Jay: Am I the only person who's wondering how we're going to get home?

Dreena: Am I the only person who thinks this is fantastic?

Mrs Wills: Well I trust this bus. Thank you, Satnav. I think we would like to go somewhere a little warmer, please.

Lee: Are you crazy? How can you trust a bus?

Wanda: He's right. Wake up, everybody: this bus has kidnapped us!

Scene Six

The bus comes out of the clouds

Sally: Well, there's no ice here. Everything is brown. Can we have a look here, please, Satnav?

Satnav: Certainly, Sally.

(The bus lands smoothly)

Mrs Wills: We've landed. Off the bus everybody. Satnav, do you have any safety reminders?

Satnav: Read the instructions.

Jay: *(Reading)* There's plenty of sun block in the glove box. If you see fire, get back in the bus. The flames move faster than you.

Lee: He really is Mr Gloom and Doom isn't he?

(They get off the bus)

Chloe: What a dump. It's just dried mud and a few trees.

Sally: Why has the bus brought us here? We were supposed to be going swimming!

Mrs Wills: I think I know. It must be part of the climate change tour. Look, there are mountains over there: this is low ground. I think this is a river or a dried-up lake. Once we could have swum here.

Chloe: So where are we?

Ahmed: Don't you watch the news? We could be in Australia, Africa, America, or even Europe. They've all had this.

Dreena: This is what I've been talking about but you don't listen. It's called a drought and it dries up the water and stops crops growing.

Ahmed: Some parts of the world are going months without rain.

Lee: That can't be right. I saw on the telly that sea levels are rising and that some cities and even countries could be flooded. So there's plenty of water around. And anyway, there have always been deserts.

Ahmed: Yes, but things are changing. Some places are getting drier. Some have got wetter.

Dreena: The weather is getting more extreme. More floods. More drought. More storms.

Jay: Why?

Ahmed: Satnav, show us more about climate change, please.

(They get back on the bus, which takes off)

Scene Seven

The bus and rocket actors should be positioned apart on the stage for this scene

Sally: Are we there yet?

Mrs Wills: I've no idea, I don't know where we're going. Can you keep the noise down? I'm trying to do the crossword.

Dreena: We're really high up in the sky. You can hardly see the Earth.

Jay: We must almost be in space.

Lee: What? The bus has gone mad.

Dreena: No, I think it's taking us to the layer of greenhouse gases up here. It keeps the Earth warm but it's getting too thick.

Jay: What do you mean?

Dreena: The carbon dioxide and other greenhouse gases rise up and gather high up in the atmosphere.

Ahmed: You know, you're to blame for some of these gases.

Lee: Are you on about car gases again?

Ahmed: No, actually. They come from eating meat.

Lee: You what?

Ahmed: We grow loads of grain – which we could eat – and we feed it to cattle. When they burp and fart–

Lee: Ha, he said fart!

Ahmed: They let out a gas called methane and it rises all the way up here with the other greenhouse gases. Like Dreena said–

Dreena: It keeps in the heat that would normally escape into space.

Ahmed: That changes the weather.

Delon: I'm bored with this.

Wanda: Let's play I spy.

Delon: OK. I spy with my little eye something beginning with C.

Wanda: Clouds.

Delon: How did you know?

Wanda: Delon, all we can see is clouds.

Sally: I can see something else. I spy with my little eye something beginning with R.

Astronaut: Five years of training and finally I can say it: Houston, we are about to leave the Earth's atmosphere. Over.

Mission Control: Roger that.

Ahmed: Raincloud.

Sally: No.

Astronaut: Er… Houston, there seems to be a bus flying by my rocket. Over.

Delon: Restaurant.

Sally: Are you serious?

Delon: No, just hungry. There's nothing but clouds out there, Sally.

Mission Control: A bus? Are you serious? Over.

Astronaut: It's painted with flowers and there are kids in it. One of them is waving at me.

Sally: You're looking out of the wrong side.

Mission Control: OK, so there's a bus flying up there with you and it's full of schoolkids. Over. *(To a colleague)* Our astronaut has flipped.

Astronaut: Oh, and there's no one driving it. The only adult is sitting near the front and seems to be doing a crossword. Over.

Sally: Do you give in? It's a rocket.

Wanda: Rocket? There isn't a rocket!

Sally: I told you, you were looking out of the wrong side. It's gone now, but there was a rocket and I waved at the man in the window.

Mission Control: Any witches on broomsticks, or unicorns out of the other window? Over.

Delon: Do you believe her?

Wanda: Not in a million years. As if there was a rocket!

Astronaut: You think I'm making this up? It was there, I tell you. Don't you believe me? Over.

Mission Control: Not in a million years. We're bringing you back down before you tell us the Moon is made of cheese. Your mission is over. Over. *(To colleague)* Switch to autopilot and bring that crazy guy back. A busload of children. What are they on, a school trip round the world? Ha ha.

(Mission control and Astronaut exit)

Act Two Scene One

The bus engine splutters and stops. The bus glides down to land in a clearing surrounded by trees

Lee: That didn't sound good. The engine cut out.

Mrs Wills: Do you think it's broken down? *(She tries to start the engine with the key. Nothing happens)* It won't start.

Lee: Great, now we're stuck in some dump with no way of getting home. Some trip this is turning out to be.

Wanda: All I can see is green.

Chloe: It looks like a jungle out there.

Dreena: It is a jungle, airhead: we're in the rainforest.

Lee: Why has it brought us here? We're not bothered about the rainforest. It's across the world from us!

Dreena: But this rainforest is important. There are millions of trees here, and they soak up carbon.

Ahmed: That's the carbon released by people like you with big flash cars and patio heaters.

40

Mrs Wills: All right, you two. We can't blame Lee on his own for global warming, can we? We're all responsible for it. Let's get out and have a look. Satnav, any safety instructions?

Satnav: *(Very faint)* Read the display.

Jay: It's hard to see. *(Reading)* I need fuel. You can get it from a farm down the track. Be careful. There's plenty of insect spray in the glove box. Don't go too near the swampy bits by the river.

Dreena: Did you say 'swampy bits' and 'river'?

Chloe: Ha! Princess Preachy has gone a funny colour. Not so sure of yourself now, are you?

Jay: Why, what's the problem?

Chloe: *(Hums the tune of 'Never Smile at a Crocodile', but stops suddenly)* Ouch! Something just bit me!

Dreena: Insects, remember? They're terrible for your skin, you know.

Jay: Come on, you two. Stop fighting and put the insect stuff on.

Mrs Wills: I'm going to take a group with me to the farm to ask for fuel. Can some of you stay here and guard the bus?

Jay: I will, I'll look after Satnav.

Chloe: I will. I'm too thirsty to go anywhere.

Dreena: I will, to make sure they don't do anything stupid.

Lee: I will, because I don't fancy the walk. I'll take care of the keys. *(He puts his feet up on a seat)*

Mrs Wills: The track goes this way. We won't be long. Be careful.

(Mrs Wills takes Ahmed, Wanda, Delon and Sally down the track, off stage)

Jay: Bye. Hey, what's that buzzing noise?

Dreena: That will be the insects, I expect.

Lee: No, it's definitely chainsaws, like in Chainsaw Fighter. There must be loads of them.

Jay: Why would there be chainsaws here?

Dreena: Deforestation. They're cutting down the trees. We have to stop them. Come on!

Lee: Hey, she's going to have a fight! This could be fun. You two stay behind and guard the bus. I'm not missing this.

(Dreena and Lee walk towards the sounds of the chainsaws. Jay and others leave the stage)

42

Do you think they'll let me have a go with a chainsaw? That would be cool.

Dreena: You are joking, aren't you? Hey, you! STOP WHAT YOU ARE DOING!

Gab: *(Enters and comes towards them)* Who are you? What are you talking about?

Dreena: You must stop cutting down those trees.

Gab: Why? Logging is my dad's job and I'm helping him.

Dreena: But the trees are important for the planet. You don't understand. They soak up carbon.

Gab: But we need the money. It's our job. And the trees will grow back.

Dreena: But that will take ages. We need to soak up the carbon now.

Gab: Well, where does all this carbon come from?

Dreena: All sorts of places – planes, cars, factories, burning coal….

Gab: And do you see any of those things round here?

Dreena: Er, no.

Gab: So who is sending out all this carbon with their planes, cars, factories and coal?

Dreena: Um, well, developed countries, I guess.

Gab: Like where you come from?

Dreena: Well, yes.

Gab: And how many trees have you planted to soak up the carbon?

Dreena: Well, I live in a flat and we haven't got a very big garden so we can't plant trees there and….

Gab: Right. So you want my dad to stop cutting down trees because of a problem that comes from your country, but you haven't actually done anything about it yourself?

Dreena: You don't understand! You're killing the planet!

Gab: It's you who doesn't understand. Anyway, you could be paying for this logging.

Lee: What do you mean?

Gab: Some of the wood is burned to make charcoal for barbecues. These trees are turned into charcoal for the Jungle World brand. Have you heard of it?

Lee: We use that. My dad says it's the best.

Gab: And the bigger pieces of wood are sold to make…

Lee: Decking?

Gab: Right.

Dreena: Like at your house, Lee.

Gab: See? Now maybe you understand better.

Dreena: Yeah, but –

Gab: Now you'd better leave because if Mr Dev finds you here, telling us to stop working, he might not stand around for a chat like me. He hasn't got very nice manners.

(Exit)

Scene Two

Meanwhile, Chloe and Jay get off the bus

Chloe: I'm so thirsty. We have to find some water. Come on.

Jay: Hey, there's a house. And wow, that lorry parked by it has the Jungle World logo. What's that doing here?

Maria: *(Comes from her house)* What are you doing?

Jay: We're looking for water. Do you have any?

Maria: Sure. Come this way.

Chloe: What's that Jungle World lorry doing here? There aren't any shops!

Maria: No, there are no shops that sell Jungle World stuff. But we make it here in the workshops.

Chloe: You work for Jungle World?

Maria: Yes. I'm on my break. Come in.

Chloe: Thanks. Hey – how come you're working? You're the same age as us and we don't work.

Maria: Everyone here has to work as soon as they can. We have to earn money somehow. Come in.

Jay: *(To Chloe)* This is such a tiny house. It's only one room.

Chloe: There's a box of Jungle World labels. Those T-shirts are like my one that got stained!

Maria: *(Hands them both a drink)* I finish off the T-shirts for Jungle World. I sew in the pretty pattern and add the labels.

Jay: Is this your house as well as your workshop?

Maria: Yes, this is my home too. Is it different to your houses?

Chloe: Well, we've got more stuff, like computers and toys.

Maria: Would you like something to eat?

Jay: No, we're fine. Is it hard work?

Maria: It's really boring, and we get paid for how many we do, not how long it takes. I get five cents for every T-shirt.

Chloe: That's nothing!

Maria: There aren't many ways to make a living in the rainforest. Beautiful scenery doesn't pay the bills!

Jay: Can't you ask for more money?

Maria: You don't know my boss! He doesn't like that kind of talk. I'm afraid I need to get back to work now.

Jay: Yes, we can see that. Thanks for the drink.

Maria: You're welcome. *(As they leave, Maria starts sewing at her machine)*

Jay: I thought I was the poor one out of us lot. But Maria has almost nothing.

Chloe: Yeah. Those Jungle World clothes don't look as stylish out here, do they?

Jay: That stuff is really expensive isn't it? Lee wears it, so it can't be cheap.

Chloe: It's pricey. The money certainly doesn't come to Maria, does it?

Jay: Hey, the chainsaws have stopped. Maybe Dreena talked them round. Let's go and find out.

(Exit)

Scene Three

Gab, Dreena and Lee are in the logging area. Mr Dev enters

Mr Dev: It's quiet! Why have you turned off the chain-saws? Don't you want to be paid this week?

Gab: It's OK, Mr Dev. We just stopped for a little while to talk to these visitors.

Mr Dev: Ah, that explains the crazy-looking bus down the track. Just right for my logs, that would be, if you took the seats out and the roof off. OK, get back to work, guys.

Dreena: Are you in charge of these chainsaws?

Mr Dev: What if I am?

Dreena: Do you know how important these trees are to the whole planet?

Mr Dev: They're important to me and my workers. Everybody has to pay their bills.

Dreena: But when you burn the trees it lets out all the carbon and that goes into the atmosphere.

Mr Dev: Ah yes, like the carbon that comes out from your bus.

Lee: Not at the moment. It's out of fuel. *(Proudly)* I'm looking after the keys.

(Chloe and Jay run up)

50

Chloe: Great, we found you. Hey, you'll never believe this: Jungle World clothes are made here. We met this girl and she works in a really small house and only gets paid a few cents for each one she finishes.

Jay: She sounded really scared of her boss – What? What's everybody staring at US for?

Mr Dev: So we've got some more little activists, have we? You've been going round stirring up trouble with my workers.

Jay: We only talked to one of them. We're not trying to make trouble.

Mr Dev: You might not be trying to, my friend, but you certainly are making trouble for me.

Dreena: But there must be better ways to make money round here. People would pay to come to see this beautiful rainforest. You could show them round.

Mr Dev: Listen, kid, it's a nice idea but a few tourists won't spend enough for all these people to live on. Now, you're starting to get on my nerves. This is private land and I want you to leave.

Chloe: Our friends went to get fuel from the farm.

Mr Dev: Go this way. It's on the same path. You'll meet them.

Dreena: But can't we stay and talk about the logging?

Mr Dev: *(Picks up a chainsaw)* I don't want you going past my workers again and upsetting them. Goodbye.

(Gab, Dreena, Chloe and Jay exit)

Scene Four

Lee hangs back from the others

Lee: Mr Dev? Can I have a word?

Mr Dev: I don't need any more lectures on doing the right thing for the planet, kid, OK? Keep moving.

Lee: No, I understand what you're doing here. So you cut down a bit of the forest but it's huge, isn't it, and there are loads more trees. Everybody has to earn a living.

Mr Dev: You talk more sense than your friend. So what did you want to talk about?

Lee: You make the Jungle World clothes here, right?

Mr Dev: Some of them.

Lee: And you make the Jungle World wood products like doors and charcoal.

Mr Dev: So?

Lee: My dad runs a really big store. What if you let us sell your products?

Mr Dev: *(Looks doubtful)* Hmm. We'll see. Write your email address here and I'll be in touch.

(Lee writes down his address)

(Seeming innocent) I saw you looking at the chainsaw. Want a go?

Lee: Yeah!

Mr Dev: Safety first. Give me those keys so they don't get in the way. Now, hold it like this.

Lee: Cool.

Mr Dev: I'll switch it on and you can cut up this log.

Lee: Yeah, goddit. *(Lee uses the chainsaw briefly)*

Mr Dev: Now you'd better join your friends.

Lee: *(Handing back the chainsaw)* Thanks. See you later!

Mr Dev: I doubt it. *(To himself)* It'll be crocodiles you'll be seeing later. As if I need a kid salesman! *(He rattles the keys to the bus)*. Now where's that can of fuel? Time to try out my new bus.

(Exit)

Scene Five

Lee catches up with Jay, Dreena and Chloe on the path

Chloe: How long do we stay on this track for? It's getting very muddy.

Dreena: I'm using this stick. We're right by a river – Mr Dev didn't say anything about that.

(Chloe starts humming 'Never Smile at a Crocodile' to herself)

Jay: Why were you palling up with Mr Dev?

Lee: He's just a businessman. He's got to make a living.

Jay: I don't trust him. I'll be glad to be on the bus and flying away from here.

Lee: The bus! He kept the keys! He conned me!

Dreena: *(Jumps)* Watch out!

Chloe: Oh. My…

Lee: *(Interrupts)* There's a crocodile behind you! Run!

Jay: Er, if we stay together, we might be safer.

Lee: They're between us already. You lot head for the trees. I'll um… I'll throw mud at their heads – it will make it harder for them to see.

(The crocodiles creep towards the children and are slowed down by Lee's mud throwing)

Scene Six

A crocodile is right in front of Dreena

Dreena: Nice crocodile. Nice crocodile. You can't eat me, I'm a vegetarian.

Chloe: Watch it!

(The crocodile leaps at Dreena and she jams the stick in its mouth)

Dreena: Hah! Can't bite me now, can you. Watch out Jay, there's one coming up behind you!

Jay: Oh no! I'm dead.

Chloe: Over here, Jay. There's room on this tree.

Jay: But the river's in the way!

Chloe: Come on Jay, you have to swim!

Lee: I can't hold them up much longer. I'll climb this tree. Swim across!

(Jay jumps in, followed by the crocodile)

Jay: *(Talking to himself)* Come on, come on, just a bit further. Feet up and kick. Fingers together and pull.

Dreena, Chloe, Lee: Keep going! Faster!

Jay: Phew! Made it!

Chloe: That's it, climb up. That was amazing! You were swimming!

Jay: *(Proudly)* Well, it's not that hard is it? You just need the motivation.

Dreena: Lee, you did a great job with the mud. Thank goodness we're all safe high up.

Lee: Hey, careful Chloe. You're on a low branch and that crocodile is right underneath you…

Chloe: This tree is so slippy – Aah! *(She falls)*

Jay: Chloe! Get up! Run, run to that bridge.

Dreena: She's lost her shoes running in that mud.

Jay: Keep going, Chloe! Oh no, it's got her!

Chloe: Argh!

(We hear screams, splashing and the buzzing of chainsaws)

Act Three Scene One

Maria's house. Maria and Gab are looking after Chloe, Dreena, Jay and Lee

Maria: Pass me that old shirt, Gab. I need to clean this foot up a bit.

Gab: Here. Take it.

Chloe: That's a Jungle World shirt! You mustn't use that – you won't get paid for it.

Maria: It's OK. It's only one shirt.

Dreena: Is she going to be all right? There's a lot of blood.

Maria: She was lucky. The crocodile only got a tiny bit of her foot.

Chloe: Hey, my wart has gone! The crocodile bit off the wart on my foot!

Dreena: It's still bleeding.

Maria: Gab, go and fetch our medicines.

Jay: There's a first-aid box in the bus. Why don't I get that?

Maria: No, it's OK. We make a lot of medicines in the rainforest.

58

Gab: A lot of natural remedies are made from bark, leaves and plants. I'll bring back something to stop the blood. *(Goes into the rainforest)*

Jay: Thanks again for saving us, Maria. How did you know where we were?

Maria: We realised that Mr Dev had sent you along the path to the crocodile swamp. We ran up with the chainsaws working and the noise frightened the crocs away.

Chloe: Hey, you know what? We did well out there.

Dreena: What do you mean?

Chloe: Well, you stood up to a crocodile and stuck a log in its mouth to jam it open.

Jay: And I swam! I really swam! And Lee, throwing mud in their eyes was a brilliant idea.

Dreena: And you even got rid of your wart, Chloe!

Chloe: Actually I was getting quite fond of it. I'd rather have a wart on my foot than a crocodile slicing my leg off.

(Gab returns with some leaves and powders. With him are Mrs Wills and the rest of the party)

Gab: I found your friends looking for their bus.

Mrs Wills: Thank goodness we are all safe. And I'm sure these nice people will help us. I expect the bus will come back when it's ready.

Maria: Yes, we can look after you for a while until you get help. Now, let's fix that foot. *(She puts powder and leaves on Chloe's wound)*

Jay: Wow! That's amazing. The bleeding stopped almost as soon as you put that stuff on.

Gab: Like I said, we get medicines from the rainforest.

Dreena: Gab, I need to talk to you. I'm really sorry I argued with you about chopping the trees down.

Gab: It's OK. We've heard the arguments before. But what else can we do for money round here?

Dreena: Well, actually I've got an idea. I wonder if – hey, what's that noise?

Scene Two

The bus drives up to the house with Mr Dev at the wheel, shrieking. The children and Mrs Wills run out of the house

Mr Dev: Make it stop! Make it stop! I've taken the keys out and the engine's still running!

Dreena: The bus has got Mr Dev!

Mr Dev: Stop, you stupid machine. Stop!

Mrs Wills: He hasn't learned about using his manners, has he?

Dreena: The bus is whizzing round in circles!

Mr Dev: Stop. I'm getting dizzy! I'm going to fall out!

Lee: Please, Satnav. Please stop. *(The bus stops)* Thank you.

Mr Dev: *(Jumps from the bus)* That thing is dangerous!

Lee: Dangerous! You were the one who sent us on the path to the crocodile swamp. We could have been killed. And you stole the keys.

Mr Dev: I forgot to give them back. And I showed you the path to your friends.

Lee: OK. Let's test that out. Bus, please take Mr Dev the same way he sent us.

(The bus starts up and beings to nudge Mr Dev in the direction of the crocodile swamp)

Mr Dev: No, no. All right, I sent you towards the crocodiles. I'm sorry.

Lee: Bus, please stop. *(The bus stops)* Thank you. Right, Mr Dev. I think we'll have our bus back. Give me the keys.

(Mr Dev throws them across)

Lee: OK, the bus is working, let's get out of here.

Dreena: Not yet. I've got a plan – I think we can help everyone here. Gab, can you get the villagers to come for a meeting?

Gab: No problem.

Lee: What are you going to do?

Dreena: We've got to help them so they don't have to chop the trees down.

Scene Three

The villagers and the children are sitting in a big circle outside Maria's house

Dreena: We understand that you have to make a living, and your trees are being sold to our country for charcoal and doors. We can't just tell you to leave the trees alone.

Gab: We want to be able to let the trees grow. This is our land and we love it.

Maria: We know it as well as you know your homes and streets. But everybody has mouths to feed.

Dreena: We've got some plans that will help us, and help you.

Jay: The first thing is we can't ask you to stop cutting down trees if we don't do our bit to help.

Ahmed: All of us who came here today should agree to try to put less carbon into the atmosphere.

Lee: But how can we do that?

Wanda: It's easy, Lee. Simple things like turning the lights off when we leave the room, and not leaving the TV on standby because it still uses electricity.

Ahmed: And we should stop wasting energy with stupid things like patio heaters – if you want to stay outside, put another jumper on.

Chloe: And we will plant more trees in our gardens and at our school.

Dreena: But the rainforest is so lovely, and so important, we need to treat it properly.

Gab: Our tribe has been doing that for thousands of years.

Maria: We know how to manage these forests so that when we cut down trees, they will be replaced.

Dreena: And we still want to trade with you, so that you have money coming in.

Jay: We noticed you have some fantastic medicines that you make from the forest. People in our country will want them. Lee's dad is a businessman and he could help to sell them.

Wanda: The rainforest is so beautiful that people will enjoy visiting it. My mum works at a travel agent, so she can help to get you customers. Maria and Gab would be the perfect tour guides here in the rainforest.

Chloe: The clothes you make are really good. But they sell for a lot of money in our country and you're paid too little. We need to work out a better deal.

Gab: So we won't have to work for Mr Dev?

Chloe: It's up to you. Mr Dev, will you pay them more?

Mr Dev: Well…

(The bus engine starts and it moves very slowly towards Mr Dev)

I can try.

Mrs Wills: I think it's time to go. We'll be in touch.

(They say their goodbyes then exit)

Scene Four

Back at school. The bus lands in the playground and the children get out. Mrs Hurst is waiting anxiously

Mrs Hurst: Oh there you are. I was getting a bit worried. The swimming trip doesn't usually last all day.

Mrs Wills: Things got a bit complicated. But we had a great trip.

Jay: And I learned to swim!

Chloe: He can swim really fast, Mrs Hurst!

Mrs Hurst: How did you do that, Jay?

Jay: It's all about motivation. If you've got an enormous crocodile snapping at your heels, you move through the water like an Olympic champion.

Mrs Hurst: Oh those plastic ones at the pool are fun, aren't they?

Chloe: Er yeah, that's right, Mrs Hurst. Oh, we brought you back something for your headache. Try this. *(She gives Mrs Hurst a paper bag)*

Mrs Hurst: Mmm. Smells lovely. I'll try it with my tea. So, Mrs Wills, how did you find the class?

Mrs Wills: Very resourceful, Mrs Hurst. In fact, I'd like to come back and help them with a few things if I may?

Mrs Hurst: Be my guest. You could take them swimming again if you like.

Mrs Wills: I'm not sure that would be a good idea.

(The bus makes a loud beeping sound and the engine roars)

Mrs Hurst: Isn't that your bus? Who's driving it?

(The bus flies into the sky leaving a huge cloud of green smoke. When it clears, there is a small camper van in its place)

What's happening?

Mrs Wills: I think the rental period must be over. That's my camper van in the playground and I have a few jobs to do today. I need to talk to my neighbour. I'll see you again. Bye!

Everyone: Bye, Mrs Wills!

Mrs Hurst: Now, we need to choose our topic for the next term. Any ideas, class?

Lee: How about the rainforest, Mrs Hurst?

The End

Exploring the play
Act One Scene One

Discussion

Lee is playing his Chainsaw Killer computer game, which is obviously quite violent. Do you think these games encourage people to be violent in real life? There are age limits to stop younger children playing games with lots of fighting in them. Do you agree with this and does it work?

Writing

How do we learn about the children's characters in this scene? Write a one-sentence character description of Lee, Jay, Ahmed, Dreena or Chloe. Read it out and say how you reached your view.

Scene Two

Discussion

Lee judges people by what car they have. What do you think different cars reveal about their owners? How do we get these views? What role do design and advertising have in this?

Scene Three

Improvisation

Mrs Wills finds her car has turned into a bus, which then starts telling her what to do. Act out these events, saying her thoughts aloud.

Scene Four

Movement

Sit in rows as if you are on a bus. Imagine it is going along a bumpy road with lots of turns. Have a leader to call out 'left' or 'right' or 'bumps'. Everybody has to move their body to suggest the journey. Try this where the leader moves, rather than talks, and everybody else copies them.

Scene Five

Tableaux

In groups, create a tableau (a 'human picture') of a glacier – a very slow moving frozen river. Then make it collapse suddenly.

Scene Six

Movement

The children land in a dried-up river. How do we behave when we are hot? Use movement and expression to show a hot environment.

Scene Seven

Improvisation

We hear the conversations of the astronaut and the children. Can you create a similar situation where two separate conversations take place and only the listener understands what is happening?

Act Two Scene One

Writing/presenting

Burning fuel releases carbon. Do some research using books and the Internet to find out how this happens and its effect on the atmosphere. Prepare a one-minute report on what you discover and present it to the class.

Scene Two

Discussion

Many cheap fashion clothes are made abroad, sometimes by young people working in poor conditions. How do you feel about buying clothing that is cheap because people who make it are paid very little? Does it matter to you or not?

Scene Three

Hotseating

Ask one or two children to think about the

character of Mr Dev. What is he like? How do you think he came to be in charge of the loggers in the rainforest? One pupil should be Mr Dev, in the hot seat, and the others should interview him and find out his background and why he continues cutting down the trees.

Scene Four

Movement and sound

Lee has a go with a chainsaw, a large and dangerous piece of machinery. Split into two groups. One acts out using a chainsaw. The other creates sound effects for it. Put the two performances together.

Scenes Five and Six

Freeze-framing

Act out the children's movements as they try to escape the crocodiles. What will their expressions be like? How could you show fear? How would they move? Ask another group how they would depict the crocodiles.

Act Three Scene One

Discussion

How have the relationships changed between Chloe, Dreena, Lee and Jay after their battle with the crocodiles? How would their body language be different to the first scene when they were at Lee's house?

Scene Two

Movement

Mr Dev is stuck on the bus as it whizzes round in circles. Act out his movements as he is thrown around. Try to show the movement of the bus as well as his reaction.

Scene Three

Writing

The children mention some of the things they can do to help release less carbon. Can you find any more ways to help? Create a poster with your ideas.

Scene Four

Tableau

The Rainforest Express bus turns back into the camper van. As a group, show this transformation. See if you can act it out while someone counts slowly to ten, so that we see the bus at 'one' and the camper van at 'ten'.